P9-DOG-584

Crocky Dilly

To Paige who drew the pictures, Tim who designed the book, and everyone else at Studio Goodwin Sturges who made Crocky Dilly's tale possible — P.S.

To my husband, Chris, and for our daughter, Charlie — P.M.

Special thanks to Peter Lacovara, archaeologist.

CROCKY DILLY

by Philemon Sturges

illustrated by Paige Miglio

Museum of Fine Arts, Boston

My name's Crocky Dilly,

I know that sounds silly,

But my Mummy, she gave me that name!

'Cause her name and her Mum's and her Mummy's Mum's Mum's

Were all exactly the same.

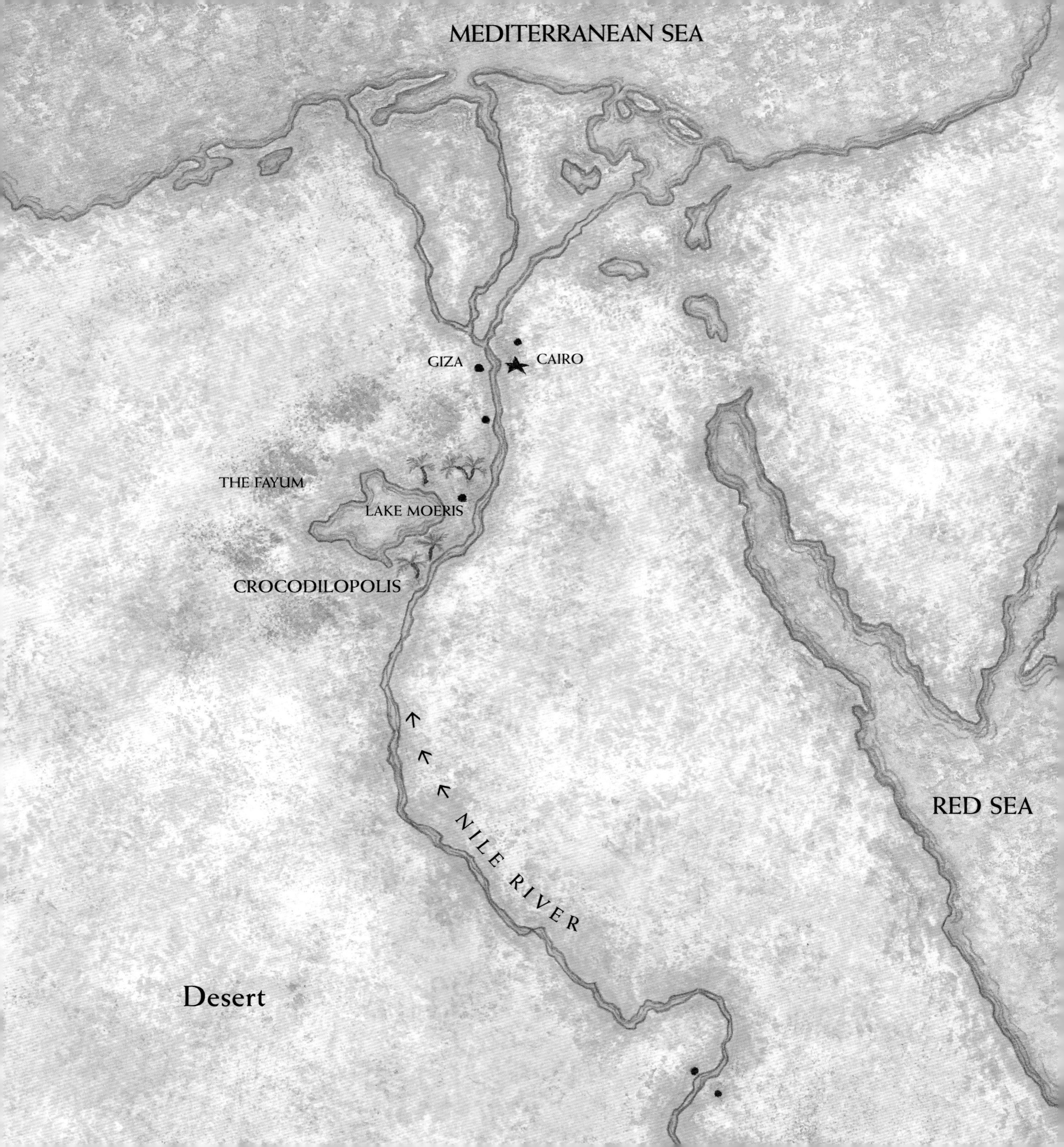
MEDITERRANEAN SEA
GIZA
CAIRO
THE FAYUM
LAKE MOERIS
CROCODILOPOLIS
NILE RIVER
RED SEA
Desert

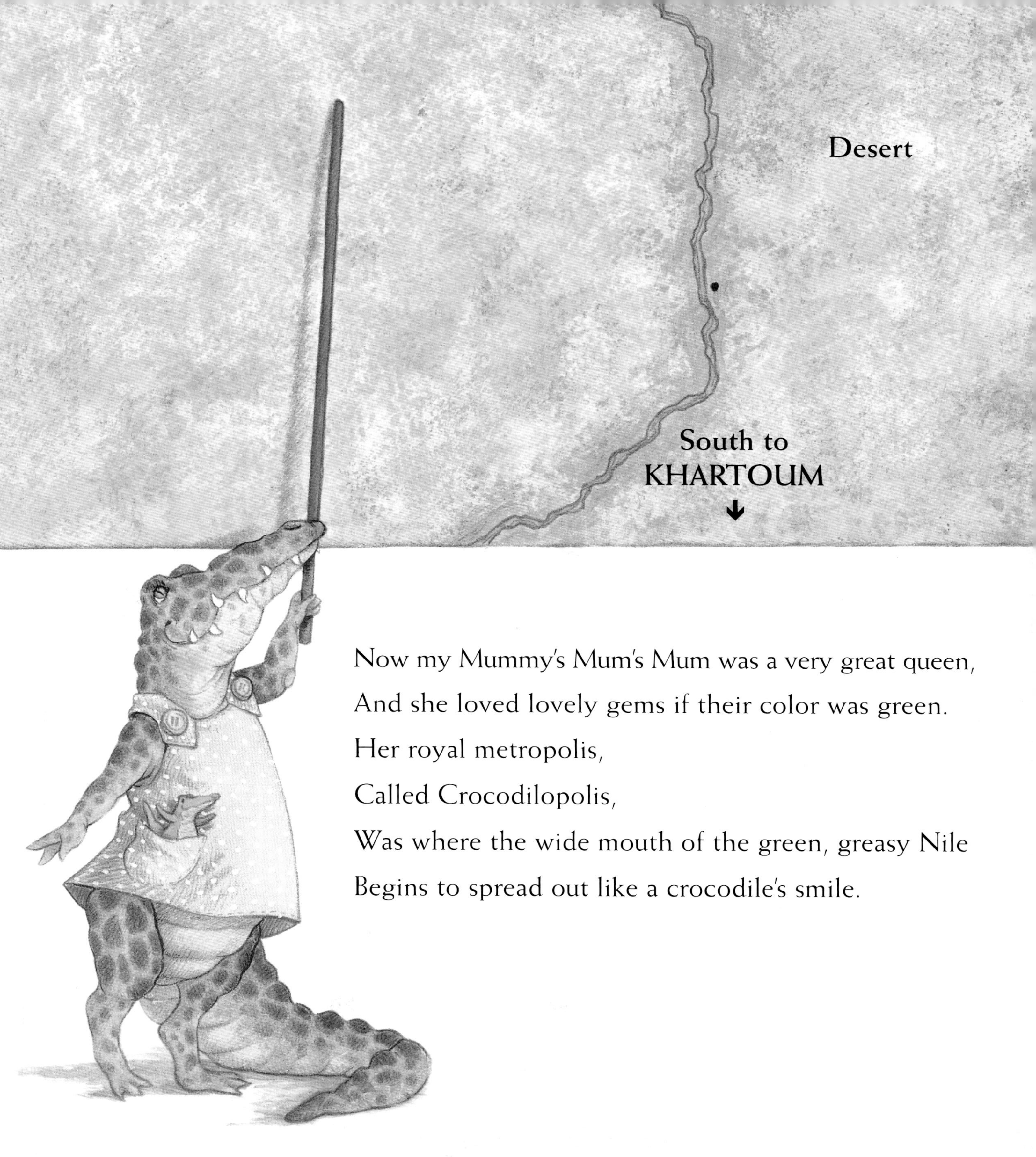

Now my Mummy's Mum's Mum was a very great queen,
And she loved lovely gems if their color was green.
Her royal metropolis,
Called Crocodilopolis,
Was where the wide mouth of the green, greasy Nile
Begins to spread out like a crocodile's smile.

My Mummy's Mum's Mum had such beautiful eyes;
Like emeralds, they'd gleam on the Nile.
One eye watched the sun, and the other the moon,
And if you came near her at midnight or noon,
She'd show you her wide, toothsome smile.

One night in a horrible hulla-ba-loo,
King Menes' big dog chased him down to the Nile.
Forgetting the crocodile's wonderful smile,
Menes leapt with a *thwack*
On her half-submerged back,
Which was NOT such a dumb thing to do!

The very brave king looked her right in the eye:
"If you save me, good Crocky," he said with a sigh,
"I'll give you the moon and I'll give you the sky.
I'll give you a city, this river to rule!"
But my Mummy's Mum's Mum just wanted a jewel.

"That's fine," said King Menes, "I'll make you an heiress
If you carry me down to a lake called Moeris."
So swishing her tail like a slithering oar,
She swam to Moeris's sacred green shore.

As Crocky swam near, Menes stood on her neck
And greeted the god of creation, Sobek.

"King Menes," he said, "you have come, I presume,
To rule the green banks of the Nile.
Your kingdom shall stretch from the swamps
of Khartoum
To the tip of her northernmost isle."

Sobek turned and looked at my Mummy's
Mum's Mum,
Who'd swum from the swamps, to the sea, and Fayum.
"Crocky," he said, "you are Queen of the Nile!
Rule over her well with your radiant smile."

"For this eye is the moon, this one is the sun…

And now, Crocky Dilly, you're my sacred one."

They both kept their word,
And as you've just heard,
The king built her a labyrinth city.
She ruled the green Nile
With her beautiful smile
And wore emeralds to make her look pretty.

She ruled the long Nile, from the swamp to the sea,
And had millions of Dillys that look just like me.
She always wore emeralds. She dressed all in green.
My Mummy's Mum's Mum was a very good queen!

When she finally died, there was sorrow and gloom
From the mouth of the Nile to the swamps of Khartoum.
She was wrapped in cloth coils,
Soaked in very rare oils,

Then, after loud wailing and speeches and cheers,
As well as a river of crocodile tears,
She was placed in a treasure-filled tomb.
And she stayed there for just about five thousand years...

'Cause my Mummy's Mum's Mum is a mummy!

CROCK

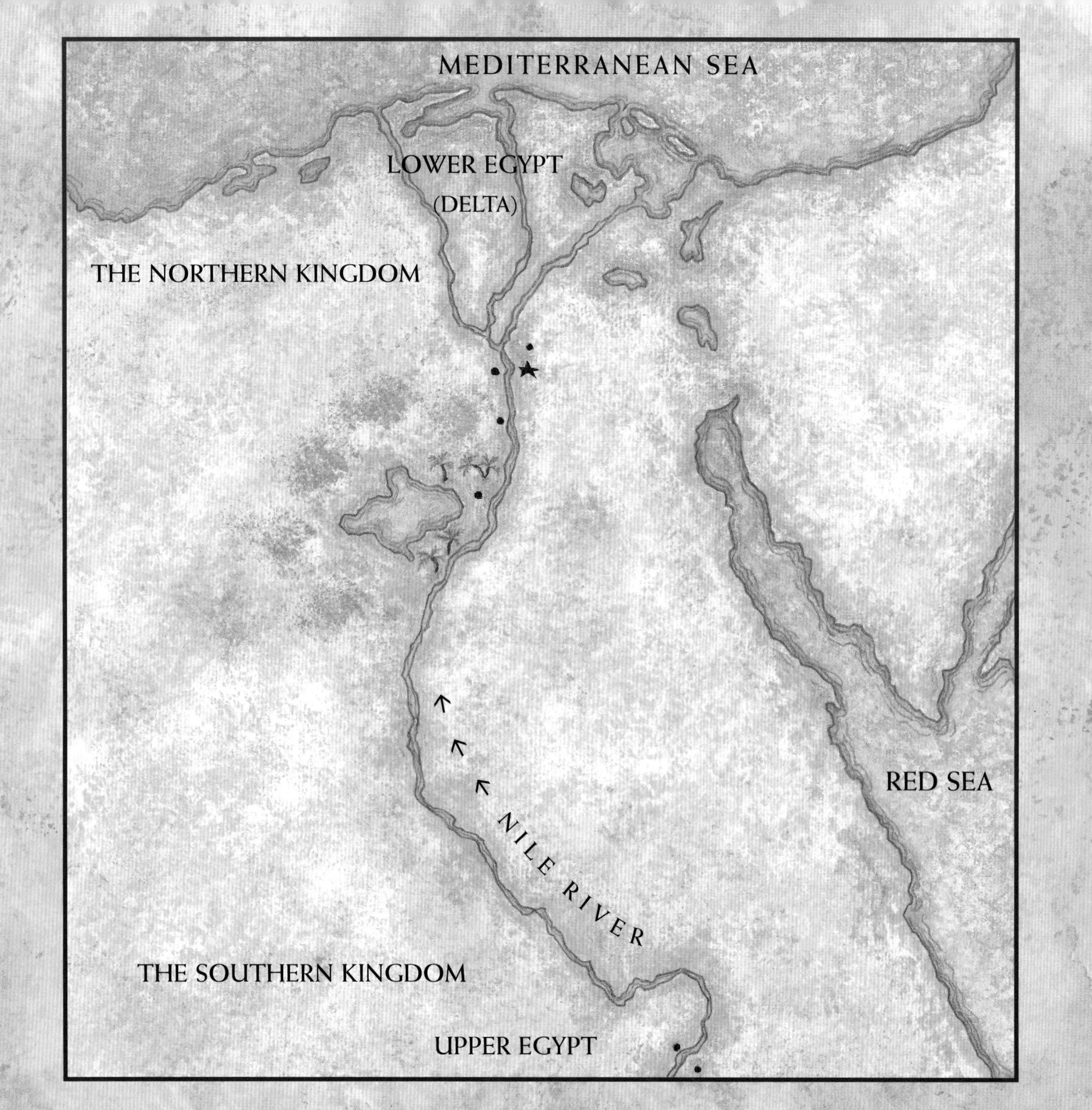

Egypt was once divided into two kingdoms. King Menes united the two kingdoms into one country.

KING MENES — pronounced *meen-eez*

Thousands of years ago in ancient Egypt there were two kingdoms. The Southern Kingdom was protected by the vulture goddess, Nekhbet. The chief of this kingdom wore a white crown.The Northern Kingdom, in the delta near the sea, was protected by the cobra goddess, Edjo. The chief of this kingdom wore a red crown. Eventually one Egyptian crown was made that combined both the red and white crowns.

King Menes (who is also called Narmer) was the chief of the Northern Kingdom. He triumphed over the South and became the first ruler of both lands. He ruled from around 3100 – 2890 B.C. and is called the first king of the 1st Dynasty.

ANIMAL MUMMIES

If you visit a museum with exhibits from Egypt, look for the animal mummies. You may find mummies of cats, baboons, ibises, rams, and of course crocodiles.

The animal mummies were often made just as carefully as human mummies with elaborate wrappings and painted and decorated cases.

These animals were usually not pets. They were sacred animals associated with certain gods, and they were buried in temples. Sometimes there were special cemeteries just for animals.

Around 450 B.C. Herodotus wrote about the pleasant lives of the crocodiles at Lake Moeris. They were given special food and were trained to be tame. He saw crocodiles wearing glass and gold earrings, and bracelets on their forefeet.

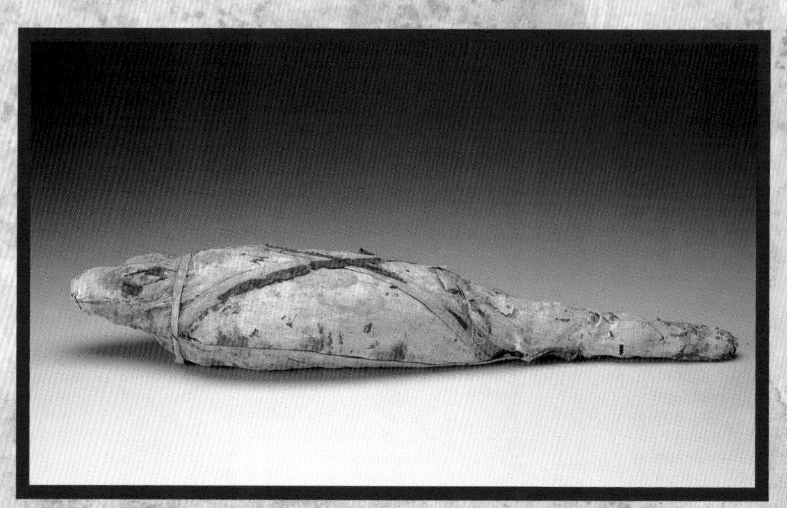

Crocodile mummy
Provenance unknown
Ptolemaic or Roman Period
Linen
Length 50 cm, width 12 cm
Hay Collection, Gift of C. Granville Way, 1872.4905

THE NILE CROCODILE

The Nile River made life in the desert possible. It provided water to drink, fish to eat, and floods for rich, wet farmland. In ancient times, there were many huge crocodiles in the Nile. The crocodiles had almost no enemies, and they could eat everything—from a tiny fish to a baby hippo.

When the Egyptians came down to the Nile, they had to be very careful. They looked to see if a crocodile was underwater near the shore. They were afraid of crocodiles, but they also respected them as rulers of the water. That is why they made them a part of their religion.

Crocodiles represented the crocodile-headed god, Sobek. He was a water god who was worshiped at the oasis at Fayum.

First published in the United States of America in 1998 by
the Museum of Fine Arts, Boston
Department of Retail Publications
295 Huntington Avenue
Boston, Massachusetts 02115

Text copyright © 1998 by Philemon Sturges
Illustrations copyright © 1998 by Paige Miglio

All rights reserved, including the right to reproduce this work in any form or means, electronic or mechanical, including photocopy and information retrieval systems, without permission in writing from the Museum of Fine Arts, Boston

10 9 8 7 6 5 4 3

ISBN 0-87846-458-1

Printed in Hong Kong